This book is dedicated to people who are working diligently on Chinese picture books. —Cao Wenxuan   For my eldest daughter, Caterpillar, and my sons Pepper and Bean, especially Bean, who produced the handwritten characters in this book. —Yu Rong

SUMMER

written by
CAO WENXUAN

illustrated by
YU RONG

[Imprint]
MAKE YOUR MARK

New York

In summer,
the burning hot sun
hangs in the sky.

Sparrows hide in the willow trees,
as does a cricket in the tall reeds.

A frog floats on a lotus leaf,
beneath the umbrella of another.
Ducks sleep with
heads tucked in wings,
beneath the cool arching bridge.
Hens doze in the dusty shade of haystacks,
and the melon farmer fans himself, under a canopy.

And by the riverbank, a girl fishes for her meal.

In summer,

the grasslands are parched.
The animals seek shelter from the sun,
their trampling feet stirring up a thick cloud of dust.

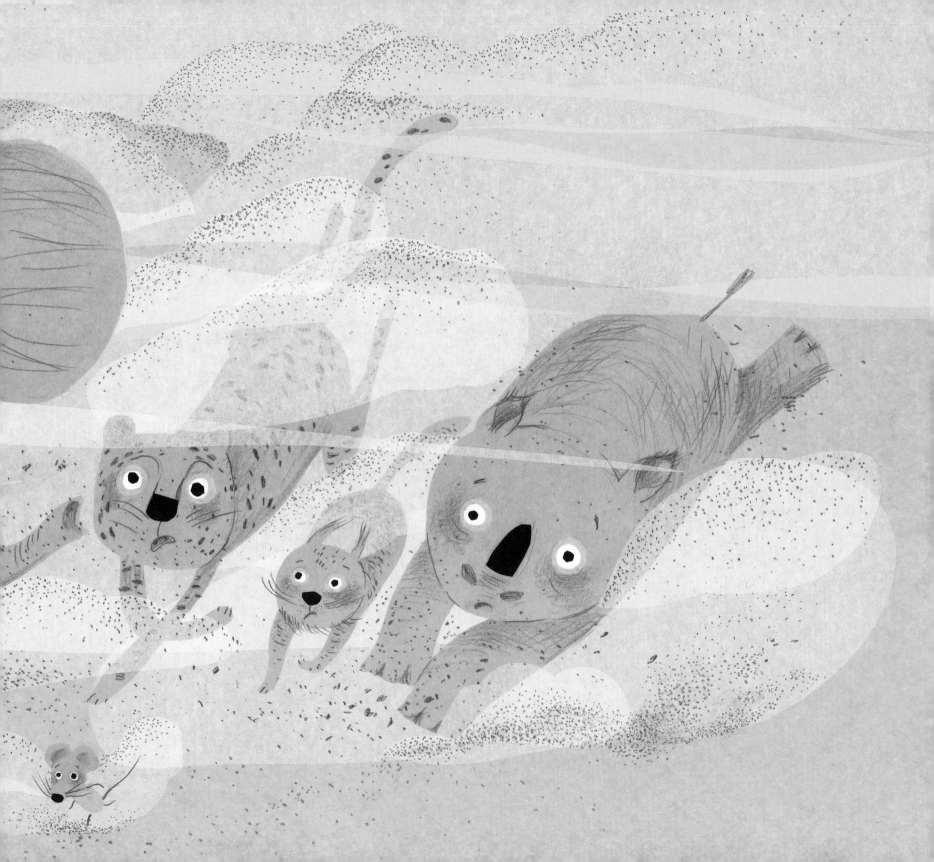

"Tree!"
the sharp-eyed jackal shrieks.
The animals dash off as fast as they can
in a mighty race to the shade of the tree.

The smallest of them all, the field mouse,
gets shoved aside.
Her little voice tries to shout,
"But it was me!
I got to the tree first!"

In Summer,

the tree is barely alive.

Only a few leaves are hanging on.

Most branches are completely bare;

with nothing growing from the twigs.

The animals' quarrel turns into a fight.
The frightened field mouse dodges to the side,
squeaking as loud as she can,
"Stop fighting! STOP IT!"

The greedy elephant is so big,
he takes the whole tree for himself.
All the animals shout at him:

"No fair! We got here first!"

The elephant gets angry, and trumpets,
"Go away! Go away!
No one wants to hear your
squabbling on such a hot day!"
He sucks up dust with his trunk and blows it onto anyone who
dares to disagree.

They glare at the elephant.

Suddenly, the animals start to laugh,
one by one, until they are all laughing.
They finally see that under the leafless tree,
there is no shade.
The elephant is sweltering in the sun,
just like the rest of them!

They laugh . . . until a scene unfolds before their eyes.
A father and his son walk across the dry grassland together.
The father's shadow completely covers the little boy.

All the animals watch in silence
as the father and son walk toward the horizon.

As the pair gets farther and farther away,
only the shape of the father can be seen.
And then he, too, disappears.

The leopard comes over,
making more shade.

In the heat of the
endless grassland,
the animals are still.

Sometime later,
the lynx says,
"Come here,
little mouse,
and rest in
my shade."

Then the jackal goes
to stand by the lynx.

Cool, dark air is brought by the brown bear.

And the rhino casts an even bigger shadow.

Flapping his large ears like fans, the elephant joins his companions at last.

And then one tiny beetle scurries over to the field mouse.

In summer, the big sun burns bright . . .

. . . until a cloud appears.

It drifts over the animals on a journey across the empty sky, but will it drift away again?

It stays.

In summer, all the friends cool off in the shade.
TOGETHER.

IMPRINT
A part of Macmillan Publishing Group, LLC
175 Fifth Avenue, New York, NY 10010

ABOUT THIS BOOK
The artwork for this book was created with cut paper and pencil.
The text was set in Sadness and Infusion, and the display type is Infusion.
The book was edited by Erin Stein and designed by Elynn Cohen.
The production was supervised by Raymond Ernesto Colón, and the production editor was Dawn Ryan.
Translation by Yan Ding, adapted by Erin Stein.

SUMMER BY CAO WENXUAN, ILLUSTRATIONS BY YU RONG. Text copyright © 2015, 2019 by Cao Wenxuan.
Illustrations copyright © 2015, 2019 by Yu Rong. All rights reserved.
Printed in China by RR Donnelley Asia Printing Solutions Ltd., Dongguan City, Guangdong Province.

Library of Congress Cataloging-in-Publication Data is available.

ISBN 978-1-250-31006-4 (hardcover)

Our books may be purchased in bulk for promotional, educational, or business use.
Please contact your local bookseller or the Macmillan Corporate and
Premium Sales Department at (800) 221-7945 ext. 5442
or by e-mail at MacmillanSpecialMarkets@macmillan.com.

Imprint logo designed by Amanda Spielman

Originally published by 21st Century Publishing Group in 2015
First Imprint edition, 2019

1 3 5 7 9 10 8 6 4 2

mackids.com

Do not steal books or shade in the sun,
or you will always sit alone as one.

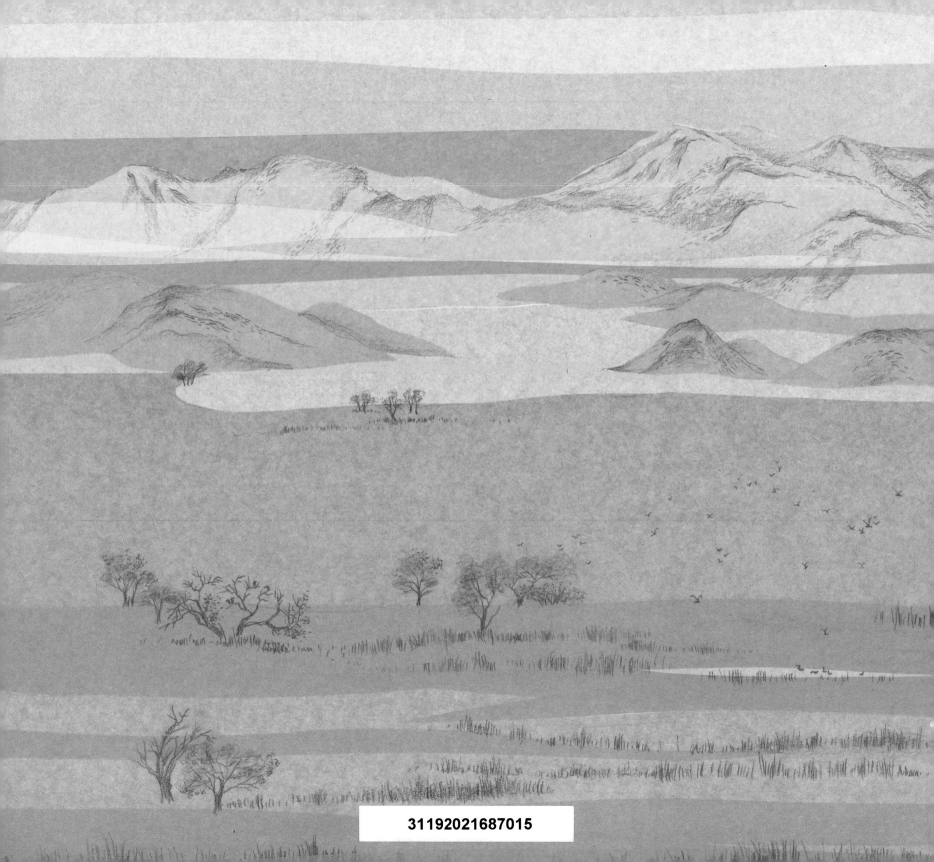